Sunny the Yellow Bunny

Written By Maria Shamkalian

Illustrated By Kim Sponaugle

Halo
PUBLISHING
INTERNATIONAL

ISBN: 978-1-61244-617-2
Library of Congress Control Number: 2018953975

Printed in the United States of America

Halo Publishing International
1100 NW Loop 410
Suite 700 - 176
San Antonio, Texas 78213
1-877-705-9647
www.halopublishing.com
contact@halopublishing.com

Thank you, everyone, who joined me in this mission of making the world a little kinder! First and foremost, I'd like to thank my family whose support and guidance encouraged me to turn my dream into an action plan. Also, I'd like to thank all those who took a stand against bullying and helped me in publishing this book:

Artem Bayadyan
Michelle Chan
Michelle Geiger
Emma and Briella Goldshteyn
Lidia Grigoryan
Pam Halter
Shaknoza Kurbanova
Nicole Kramer
Anthony and Matthew Marciano
Gita Minkovich
Sophia Onishchenko
Andrey Pak
Radek and Elita Pawlowski
Rafael, Robert and Albert Petrossian
Esther Pukhovich
Nicole and Michael Sharkov
Emilie Swerdlow
Isabella and Ornella Talapan
John Woods
Nathan and Zachary Yashin
Gabi and Liza Zanfir
Liam Zlatkovskiy

Sunny is a friendly bunny.
He is nice and he is funny.
He likes carrots, nuts,
and hay,
And eats healthy
every day.

Every day he cleans his room,
Helps his baby brother groom.
Helps his mom around the house,
Walks and feeds his neighbor's mouse.

Helps his father cut the grass,
Does his homework after class.
Never argues or offends,
But he used to have no friends.

6

It is not because he's shy,
"But then why?" you ask me,
"Why?"

"What's the reason?"
There is one:
He is yellow,
like the sun.

8

He was not allowed to play,
Just because he isn't gray.
Isn't white, or black, or brown,
So it made the bunnies frown.

Every time they said the same,
"We won't let you join the game.
Only normal bunnies can,
Be a part of our clan.

You don't look like us at all,
So, you can't play with the ball.
Can't play tag or hide-and-seek,
You are weird. You're a freak."

Sunny ran away and cried,
In his room where he could hide.
Where he would not get the looks,
And his only friends were books.

He told Mom, "This isn't right!
Can't you dye my fur to white?"
But his mommy calmly said,
"You're not strange and you're not bad."

"Why do kids call me a freak?"
"You were simply born unique.
Whether fur is real or dyed,
It's important what's inside.

No one's perfect, never was,
Every bunny has his flaws.
Friends don't judge you based on fur."
Sunny looked with hope at her.

Mommy tightly hugged her son,
And then told him, "You are fun.
You are smart and you are nice,
Let me give you some advice."

"Show them who you really are,
You're a winner! You're a star!
You are helpful! You are kind,
Such a friend is hard to find!"

14

Sunny smiled and hugged his mom,
In her arms he felt so calm.
And surrounded by her care,
He felt thankful she was there.

"Since my family is near,
There is nothing I should fear.
I should see my fur as strength,
Both its color and its length.

Love myself the way I am,
Every inch and every gram.
And before the weekend ends,
I will try to make some friends!"

Sunny's self-esteem was healed,
So, he hopped into the field.
Towards the bunnies in the hay,
Hoping they would let him play.

Suddenly, he hopped so high,
That an eagle hovered by.
Sunny cried, "An eagle! Hide!
Scary claws and wings so wide!

He is looking what to eat,
Do not be his evening treat!
Do not make it to his plate,
Hurry! Hide before it's late!"

18

Sunny's cry the bunnies heard,
"Should we trust that yellow nerd?"
Bunnies thought that Sunny lied,
And decided not to hide.

Sunny hopped a little higher,
And he screamed, "I'm not a liar!
If you do not hide away,
You'll become the eagle's prey!"

They got shocked he jumped so high,
"Maybe we should trust this guy."
All but one got scared a bit,
And went hiding in a pit.

But the brave one smirked and said,
"Silly bunnies, go ahead!
Trust the freak and hide away,
Waste a perfect, sunny day."

Suddenly the eagle's claws,
Picked him up from where he was.
"Acting brave, you silly hare?
Hope you like the open air!"

"I'm a rabbit, not a hare!"
"Trust me, schnitzel, I don't care.
For my kids you're just enough,
Even with your extra fluff.

Anyway, it's time to fly,
You can say your last goodbye.
You're a loser, I'm a winner.
You will make a lovely dinner!"

Suddenly he heard the scream,
"Hey! Forget your cruel scheme.
Or I'll bite you very hard!"
Sunny caught the bird off guard.

"Fine, I will! I'll let him go,
Yet I would, just so you know,
Eat you, too, without a blink,
But you're poisonous I think."

"Fly away and don't come back,
Or with poison I'll attack!"

When the eagle was long gone,
Bunnies gathered on the lawn.

"Sunny! Wow! How did you win?
Is there poison in your skin?"

"Did you bite him like a ferret?
Did you offer him a carrot?"

"Did you use some magic words?
Do you know a spell for birds?
Maybe you're his distant kin?
Tell us, please, how did you win?"

"There's no poison and no bite,
I just knew I had to fight.
But I'm just like all of you,
I eat grass and I drink dew.

Just like you, I hop around,
I'm afraid of every sound.
I love carrots, nuts and hay,
And I also like to play."

"Yes, we really are the same.
Please, forgive us. What a shame!
We made always such a fuss,
When you're really one of us.

Yellow, brown, black or white,
Judging others isn't right.
But it took us way too long
To admit that we were wrong."

Sunny came to Mom that night,
"Mom, you helped us all unite!
Every bunny in the town
Looks at me without a frown."

"Now I have a lot of friends,
But as this adventure ends
I have grown to understand,
Fur does not define a friend."

Discussion Questions

1) How can you describe Sunny?

2) Why did Sunny have no friends?

3) What do you think of the other bunnies' behavior?

4) How did they make Sunny feel?

5) What would you say to the other bunnies?

6) Who helped Sunny feel better?

7) What did mom teach Sunny?

8) Why did Sunny save the other bunnies from the eagle?

9) What did Sunny teach the other bunnies?

10) What did Sunny's story teach you?

11) How can people be different?

12) How are people all alike?

13) Do you have friends who are different than you? How are they different?

14) How should we treat each other, no matter how different we are?

Classroom Activities:

1) Make paper bunny ears out of paper plates and have children color them. Everyone should get a different but realistic color. One child should get a bright yellow set of bunny ears. Have him come to the middle of the room and ask other bunnies what they should have done in the story differently. (One of the answers should be about letting Sunny play ball with them.) Then have everyone stand in a circle and throw the ball to each other. The person who catches must say a word that describes a good person (kind, nice, friend, love, etc.)

2) Have children learn the lines and reenact the story for parents. Encourage families to study lines with children at home while discussing the importance of loving yourself for who you are and treating others kindly. Spend some time daily practicing in class. One of the parents can be the narrator, one boy can be Sunny, one girl can be Mom, another boy can be Eagle, one more kid can be the rebellious bunny, and the rest can be other bunnies.

3) Divide children into pairs by their differences (White and Asian, tall and short, glasses and no glasses, girl and boy, etc.) and ask children to raise hands when they like something that you name (waterparks, dogs, cats, riding a bicycle, drawing, etc.). As soon as two people from the same pair raise their hands, accentuate that even though they look different, they have a lot in common. Go through every pair to make everyone feel recognized. If it is an odd number of kids, have three children in a group (ex. three different races, heights, or hair colors)

Worksheet Activities:

1) Connect the dots. Color the picture.
Whom do you see on the picture?
How did Mom help Sunny?
Describe someone in your life who
makes you feel special and whom
you can always talk to.

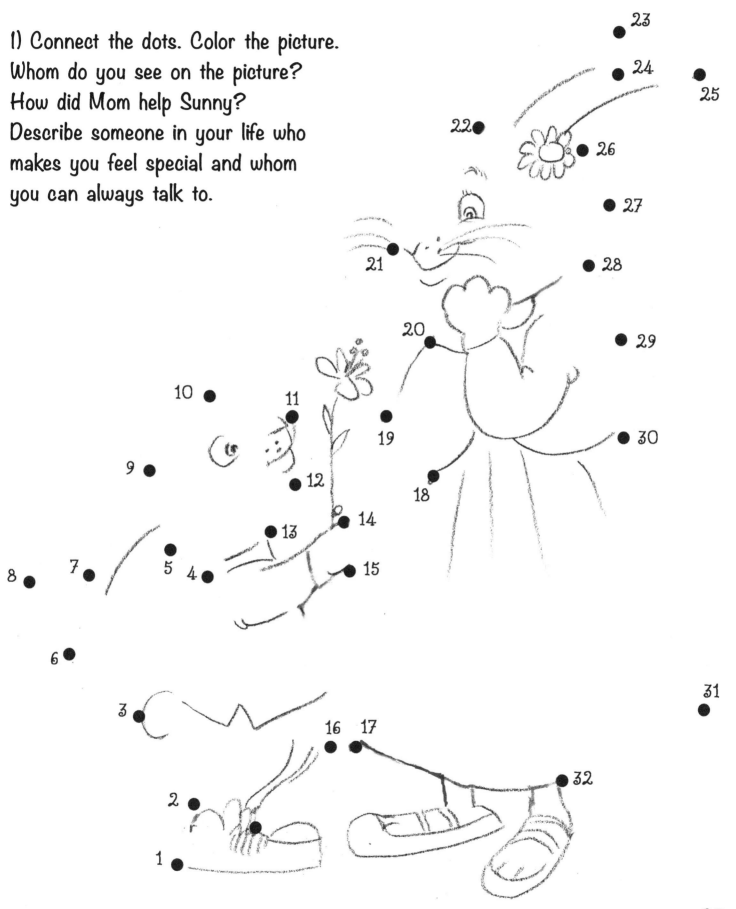

2) How many bunnies are in the picture?

How are these bunnies different?

How are these bunnies alike?

Is there anything you don't like on this picture?

How would you make that bunny feel better?

3) Color the bunnies. What makes these bunnies different? What makes them the same? Why do you think they look different? Have you ever met anyone who looks like any of these bunnies? When you do, what do you want to ask them? What would you like to learn about them and their countries? (Top row: Dutch, Inuit – Eskimo, Ukrainian, Indian, Bolivian. Bottom row: Nigerian, Native American, Scottish, Japanese) Teacher/Parent should research the answers to the questions and discuss them with the child the following day.

CPSIA information can be obtained
at www.ICGtesting.com
Printed in the USA
BVHW02s0106200818
525043BV00003B/5/P